For Frank
"Frank 'n Sense and Mirth"

First published in Great Britain in 2004
by Zero To Ten,
part of Evans Publishing Group
2A Portman Mansions
Chiltern Street
London W1U 6NR

British Library Cataloguing in Publication Data
Clibbon, Meg
Magical Christmas
1. Christmas - Pictorial works - Juvenile literature
I. Title
394.2'663

ISBN 1 84089 377 X

Printed in China

Magical Christmas

Merry Meg
and
Lucy Longstockings

Introduction

Christmas is a time of magic and splendour – the time when the birth of Jesus is celebrated. Everyone catches the excitement of preparing and enjoying this favourite festival. But why do we do certain things, eat certain things and decorate our houses in particular ways? This book will tell you all you need to know about how Christmas is the most magical time of all the year.

Winter Festivals

Long, long ago when people lived in huts and didn't have electricity, computer games or even flushing lavatories, the winters were long, dark and rather frightening. People worried that the sun, with its warmth and light, might disappear for good. Great bonfires were lit to encourage the sun to return to its full strength – there was dancing, singing and lots of parties and merrymaking.

Well, it must have worked because the sun did come back, and always has done. Some people think this is because of science and not parties, but you can't be too careful. The first Christians trying to find a good time to celebrate Jesus's birthday chose the middle of winter – they wanted Christ's message to bring light to the darkness of the world. They also didn't want to miss out on a good party!

★ The First Christmas Story ★

Two thousand years ago the Holy Land was ruled by the Romans.
The Romans said that everyone had to go back to the village of their
birth to be counted for a census. A man called Joseph lived in Nazareth,
in the north of the Holy Land. He had a wife called Mary, and she
was pregnant. They had to travel to Bethlehem, the village in the south
where he was born. It was a long, hot and bumpy journey and when
they finally got to Bethlehem Mary was dying for a cup of tea. But there
were no beds left anywhere and no tea either. At last, tired and
desperate, they found a stable next to an inn.
That is where Mary had her baby – Jesus.

There were no doctors, nurses or midwives at all but just the soft breath of the animals in the stable and a manger full of sweet-smelling hay as a cradle for the baby. Poor Mary had coped with a long journey on a donkey's back, rejection by endless innkeepers, giving birth in a draughty stable and not even a decent cradle. It is amazing what a mother can do! The baby Jesus lay in a manger and a star shone brightly overhead.

Presents for the Baby

When Jesus was born a whole host of angels came flying out of Heaven with the good news. The first people they spoke to were some poor shepherds on the hillside near the village. After they had got over the shock of seeing the angels, the shepherds took simple gifts to the baby. Later, three Kings following the star over the stable found the baby and gave him presents of gold, frankincense and myrrh. Since then, whether you are rich or poor, giving and receiving presents has been an important part of Christmas.

Presents

You rattle them and shake them; you prod them and poke them trying to guess what is inside. They are wrapped up in coloured paper and tied with ribbons and bows. Presents are given out by special people like Father Christmas, the youngest member of the family or by Christmas elves. Of course, once you have opened your presents you have to write the thank you letters. Don't leave it too long!

Saint Nicholas

Saint Nicholas was a good bishop who lived over a thousand years ago in what is now Turkey. Many stories were told of his kindness, especially to children. One night he went to the house of a very poor man who had three little girls, and secretly he put three sacks of gold by the house, one for each little girl. He is now thought of as the patron saint of children. Many countries celebrate Saint Nicholas' Day, December 6th, by placing shoes by the fireplace at night with hay for his horse. Good children find the shoe full of sweets in the morning.

Father Christmas or Santa Claus

Father Christmas is a large, jolly man who laughs loudly.
He brings presents for good children after they have gone to
bed on Christmas Eve. He wears a fur-trimmed robe and
rides a sleigh pulled by reindeer. He doesn't mind if people
leave a mince pie and a glass of sherry out for him.

Where Santa Lives

Santa lives in a lovely house made
out of pine logs. Mother Christmas
throws sweetly scented fir cones onto
the fire to keep it toasty and warm.
Santa has big woolly slippers to put on
when he takes off his boots. Next door
is the toy factory where busy little elves
and gnomes work hard all year to make
sure that Santa's sack is full on
Christmas Eve. Outside, the reindeer
keep fit by prancing on the frosty fields
and can't wait to pull the sleigh.

A Letter to Santa

Santa likes to receive letters – especially from children who are not too greedy.

Dear Santa

I have been good all year. I want:
a computer, a new bike, a CD player, a new skateboard
clothes on p. 64 of catalogue - size 8, loads of sweets

Love from . . .

P.S. Mum and Dad have told me not to be greedy.
Let's compromise. Please may I have a football and some
sweets? I will try to be good but I can't promise.

The best way to send your letter is up the chimney but the post works, too. Address your letter to: Santa Claus, Lapland, North Pole. Always show letters for Santa to your parents before sending – it really helps.

A Christmas Assortment

Here are some of the things we think of at Christmas time . . .

Advent

Advent is the season before Christmas. It can be hard to wait for Christmas so it helps to have a calendar with little windows to open each day. There is a little picture or chocolate behind the window. Don't open all the windows at once or the grown-ups will be cross and it is essential not to make grown-ups cross before Christmas.

Cards

During Advent cards are sent to friends and family to wish them a Happy Christmas. You will always get one from someone you had forgotten to send one to. Some people include letters saying what exciting and extraordinary things they have been up to.

Carols

A carol used to be a dance but now it is a happy Christmas song, sometimes sung around the streets. Naughty children change the words when they think nobody will notice. But they do.

Crackers

Crackers are long paper parcels that explode when you pull them. Inside are ridiculous hats, silly jokes and useless presents but they are great fun.

Stockings

In some places children hang out stockings on Christmas Eve. Good children's stockings will be full of sweets or presents in the morning. Amazingly even very naughty children seem to get full stockings, too!

Snow

Everyone likes to have a white Christmas, but only some people can. Even in hot deserts people put pretend snow in their windows.

Christmas Decorations

Festive occasions are made even more special when we use decorations – and at Christmas the decorations are truly magical. Christmas decorations are supposed to be put up the week before Christmas and come down on Twelfth Night (January 5th). So why do they start appearing in October?

Christmas Trees

In snowy northern lands where the sun shines weakly and remains hidden for half the year, evergreen trees are planted beside the door as a sign of hope that new life will come again with the spring. This is why we have Christmas trees.

Stars

Long ago, a wonderful star bigger than all the rest appeared in the sky over the stable in Bethlehem. Three kings followed the star across deserts and mountains and it led them to the stable in Bethlehem. This is why stars are especially magical at Christmas. Some people say that if you wish upon a star your dreams come true.

Candles

A candle flame is a little light that shines and glows and chases darkness away. Candles look lovely as well. Don't forget, though, that they have flames that can burn you or set fire to all the other decorations.

The Christmas Fairy

Most homes have a Christmas Fairy who spends most of her life in a box in the attic. When Christmas comes around this fairy is put on top of the Christmas tree. Most fairies have light airy dresses, sparkling wings and wands with stars. However some Christmas fairies are elderly creatures with crumpled frocks and wonky wands. But they too are much loved.

Festive Food

Grown-ups behave strangely about food at Christmas. They go on diets before Christmas so they can squeeze into their party clothes, then eat and drink far too much during Christmas and afterwards join gyms and go on diets again. Children are much more sensible and eat just the right amounts of their favourite foods. They can choose from: roast turkey, roast potatoes, chestnut stuffing, bread sauce, mince pies, chocolate truffles, ice cream, cheese cake, sweets, creamy cakes, Christmas pudding, Christmas cake, gravy and Yorkshire puddings and more chocolate truffles. Strangely, Brussels sprouts seem to get left at the side of their plates. Different countries enjoy different traditional foods but whatever the country and whatever the food, Christmas is for sharing and appreciating good things to eat.

Christmas Customs

In Spain the Three Kings deliver presents on January 6th. They arrive by boat.

In Sweden a Christmas gnome lives under the floorboards and gives out presents on Christmas Eve.

Dutch children put hay and sugar inside a shoe for Santa's horse.

In Mexico two children going to a crib service had only flowers to give. These flowers turned red and looked like stars – poinsettias.

In England the day after Christmas is called Boxing Day. It gets its name because a Christmas 'box' of money was given to servants on this day long ago.

Saint Basil gives Greek children presents on 1st January. He looks like St Nicholas.

Father Christmas only brings presents to children when they are asleep – and only if they have been good!

If you stand under a branch of mistletoe someone may kiss you.

Famous Christmas Stories

The Little Match Girl by Hans Christian Andersen

Not all Christmas stories are happy. In this story a poor girl is sent out to sell matches on a cold snowy night. As the night gets colder she strikes matches to try to keep warm. Each match gives her a lovely dream picture. Finally, her last match gives her a vision of a happy land where her dead grandmother lives. In the morning her frozen body is found by passers-by but her spirit is warm and safe with her dear grandmother.

A Christmas Carol by Charles Dickens

Ebenezer Scrooge is a miserly old man with no friends who hates Christmas. Through a series of strange visions he realises what a truly happy time it can be so he changes and becomes generous, kindly and jolly.

The Legend of the Fir Tree

There is a legend that all living creatures wanted to go to Bethlehem with a gift for baby Jesus. The fir tree was sad because he had nothing to give. All he could do was stand by the stable door and look in. But the Christmas angel brought down a cluster of shining stars from the night sky and sprinkled them on the branches of the fir tree. Baby Jesus looked at the little fir tree all covered with little stars and smiled.

The Nutcracker

by Piotr Tchaikovsky

Tchaikovsky's famous ballet is about a little girl called Clara who is given a magical wooden nutcracker by her mysterious godfather on Christmas Eve. After everyone has gone to bed Clara falls asleep beneath the Christmas Tree. The nutcracker turns into a Prince who takes her on a wonderful journey through a world of dancing toys, soldier mice, sugar plum fairies and snowflakes.

Making and Giving

At this special time of the year we think a lot about giving and receiving presents. You can make it even more special with a little extra thought. Think about the lonely lady nearby who might be on her own. Could you give her a card? Think about sharing some of your time with friends to make and wrap presents. It is more fun that way. It is even more fun making home-made sweets to give as gifts. Christmas decorations can be handmade, too. Giving really is as much fun as receiving. Always remember that the art of receiving is to look pleased on the outside, even if you are a bit disappointed on the inside. Oh, and those thank you letters. Yes, they can be a chore but they have to be done if you expect to have presents next year! They are always appreciated and they are part of a sharing, giving and loving Christmas time.

Make sure a grown up helps you with these recipes.

Peppermint Stars

What you need:
450 g royal icing sugar, lemon juice,
peppermint essence, silver sugar balls,
star-shaped pastry cutter

Put the icing sugar into a bowl. Add a few drops of
lemon juice and a few drops of peppermint essence.
Slowly add hot water drop by drop and stir with a spoon until you
have a soft lump. Roll out the mixture and cut into star shapes.
Decorate with the silver balls.

Chocolate Marshmallows

What you need:
glacé cherries, angelica, large marshmallows, chocolate

Cut the cherries and angelica into pieces so they look like
evergreen leaves and berries. Melt the chocolate in a bowl over
very hot water. Dip each marshmallow in the chocolate. Arrange
the leaves and berries on the top while the chocolate is still warm.

Magical Christmas

Christmas is the most magical time of the year but the magic cannot be found in heaps of expensive presents or extravagant parties or shops playing the same tunes over and over again. No – magic is far more mysterious than that.

Perhaps you have turned a corner in a dark street and suddenly seen the twinkling lights of a Christmas tree shining in a window.

Perhaps you have torn back the wrapping paper of a parcel and found the very thing you had hoped for and waited for.

Perhaps you have sat round a table laden with festive food and seen the faces of all your favourite people smiling and happy.

Perhaps you have woken up very early in the morning with the sound of sleigh bells in your ears and a stocking-shaped lump at the end of the bed which crackles with paper and smells of tangerines.

If you have felt any of these things then you have felt the magic of Christmas.